OLIVIA™
Plants a Garden

adapted by Emily Sollinger
based on the screenplay written by Rachel Ruderman
and Laurie Israel
illustrated by Jared Osterhold

Ready-to-Read

Simon Spotlight
New York   London   Toronto   Sydney

"It is springtime, children!"
says Mrs. Hoggenmuller.
"We will plant our own gardens.

"Each student will get
a packet of seeds.
You will plant
the seeds at home."

"What will we grow?"
asks Olivia.
"Sprouts, herbs, flowers,
and beans,"
says Mrs. Hoggenmuller.
"Come choose your seeds!"

"What kind of seeds
are these?" asks Olivia.
"I do not know,"
says Mrs. Hoggenmuller.

"These are surprise seeds."

At home Olivia digs in her yard.
Perry helps her dig.

"This is going to be the best surprise garden ever," she tells Julian.

"Did you know that talking to plants can help them grow faster?" asks Father.

"I can do that!" says Olivia.

"Hello, plants," says Olivia.
"I hope that you grow
so I will know what you are."

Olivia tells her plants
lots of stories.
She shows her plants
how she rides a scooter.
She sings songs to her
plants.

Oh no!
Perry is digging a hole
right where Olivia planted
her seeds.

"Oh, Perry!" says Olivia.
"I will just have to
plant more seeds.
And I will have to be even
more patient."

"Look!" says Olivia.
She holds up a bone.
"I think it is a
dinosaur bone."

"I am not sure," says Julian.

"I found a dinosaur bone
in my garden,"
says Olivia at school.
"I do not think that is

a dinosaur bone,"
says Mrs. Hoggenmuller.
"I think it is a dog toy.
Look! It is attracting flies."

Back at her house,
Olivia checks on her plants.
"My surprise seeds have
grown into surprise plants!"

All of the children bring
their plants to school.
"This is my surprise plant!"
says Olivia.
Snap!
Olivia's plant closes around
a fly.

"That is a Venus flytrap,"
says Mrs. Hoggenmuller.
"I will call it a surprise plant,"
says Olivia.
"That fly sure looked
surprised!"

"You did a wonderful job with your garden," says Father at bedtime. "I do not think we will have any more flies," says Olivia. "Good night, Olivia!"

OLIVIA™
Becomes a Vet

adapted by Alex Harvey
based on the screenplay written by Patricia Resnick
illustrated by Jared Osterhold

Ready-to-Read

Simon Spotlight
New York   London   Toronto   Sydney

"Bernie might be sick,"
Julian tells Olivia. "He will
not eat. I keep giving him
flies, but he just sits there."

"I know what to do,"
says Olivia.

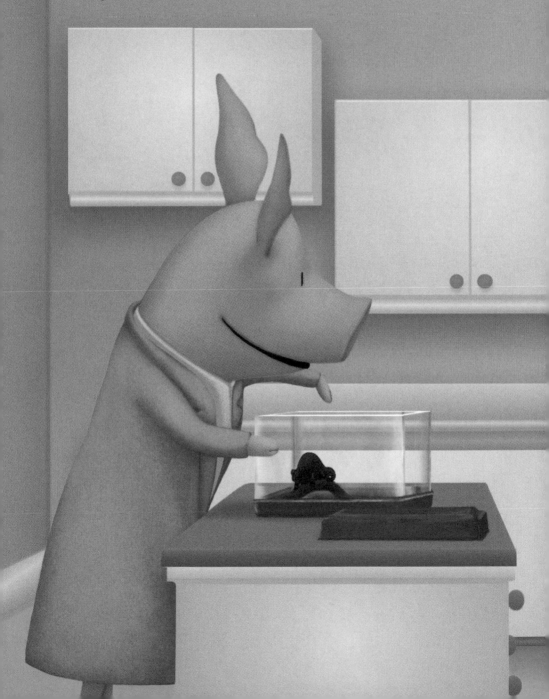

They take Bernie
to the vet for a checkup.
"What do you feed him?"
asks the vet.
"Flies," Julian says.

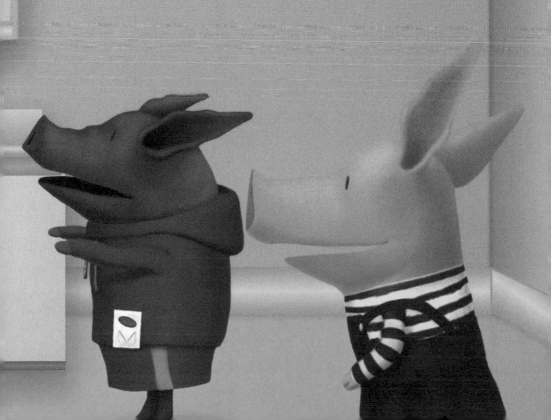

The vet nods her head. "I think I know what is wrong," she says. "I will be right back."

"Do not worry, Bernie,"
Julian tells his lizard.
"She is a very good doctor."

When the vet returns,
she feeds him a cricket.
And Bernie eats it!

"I think Bernie was bored just eating flies," the vet explains.

When Olivia gets home
she tells her mom
she wants to be a vet.
"That is wonderful,"
Mom says.

Olivia decides to start
right away.
She gets her vet bag
and instruments.

"How do you feel, Perry?"
she asks her dog.
"Hmm . . . cold nose,"
says Olivia.
"That is a good sign."

But before Olivia can do anything else, Perry runs away!

"Perry, you are not done with your checkup!"

Then Olivia decides that Edwin has a pretend illness. "You have furry-foot-itis," she says. "You need an ice pack."

Olivia begins to dream about her life as a vet. "Here is the problem," she tells a lion. "It was your sweet tooth!"

"Come on and blow!"
she says to an elephant.
"You will feel better."
"I have something to
fix you up," she tells
a camel. "Honey!"

The camel is very thankful.

"I feel better!" it says.

"Olivia is the best vet
ever!"

When Olivia finds Perry,
he has red sticky jam on
him.

"You must have strawberry
jam disease," Olivia says.

Olivia and Ian wash
Perry, and the jam
comes right off.
"You are cured, Perry!"
Olivia says.

Just then Olivia's mom says
that Edwin had an accident.
"Was it a little puddle under
the table?" asks Olivia.

"Yes," Mom says.

"Oh, it was just water from the ice pack," Olivia says.

At night Olivia's mom
tucks her in.
Mom starts to say,
"You are a special—"

"Vet?" says Olivia.

"Girl," Mom says.

"Good night, Olivia."

OLIVIA™
and Her Ducklings

adapted by Veera Hiranandani
based on the screenplay written by Eryk Casemiro and Kate Boutiler
illustrated by Shane L. Johnson

Ready-to-Read

Simon Spotlight
New York   London   Toronto   Sydney

Olivia is painting a picture
of Ian.

But Ian will not stand still.

He has an itchy nose.

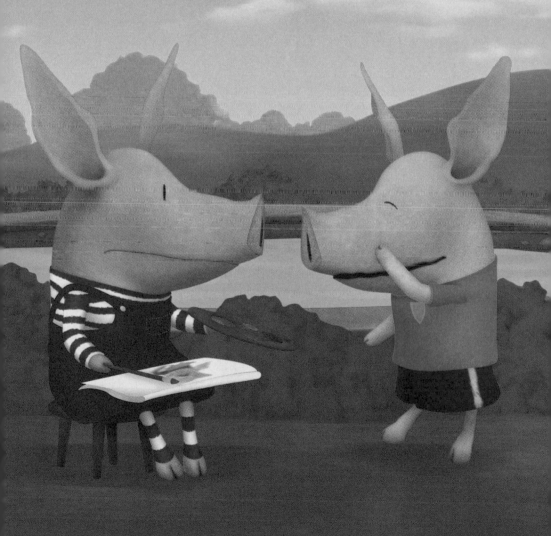

Olivia looks for something
else to paint.

She sees some ducks.

Maybe she can paint
a picture of them.

"Poor little ducks,"
says Olivia.

"They want their mother."

The ducks cannot climb
the hill.
Olivia and Ian help them.

"Come on, ducks!" says Olivia.

"Quack!" says Ian.

They did it!

Olivia wants to stay

with the ducks.

But it is time to go home.

"Good-bye, ducks!"

says Olivia.

At home, Olivia paints
a picture of flowers.
She paints her flowers
red, yellow, and pink.

Quack!

"Very funny, Ian. Please stop," says Olivia.

"Stop what?" asks Ian.

"Look!" says Olivia.

"The ducks followed us home!"

"I guess they really, really like me!" Olivia says.

"Quack!" say the ducks.

Olivia's mom sees the ducks.
"Can we keep them?"
asks Olivia.

"I'm sorry, Olivia.
The pond is their home,"
says her mom.

"The ducks have to
go back in the morning,"
her mom says.

At least the ducks can stay
for a little while.
"Who wants to play
hide-and-seek?"
Olivia asks.

"I do!" says Ian.
"Do not look behind
the piano!"
Olivia shuts her eyes.
She counts to three.

Olivia looks in the kitchen.
She does not see any ducks.

Olivia looks in the
living room.
But she does not see
any ducks.

Olivia cannot find
the ducks.
"Ian! Please help
me!" calls Olivia.

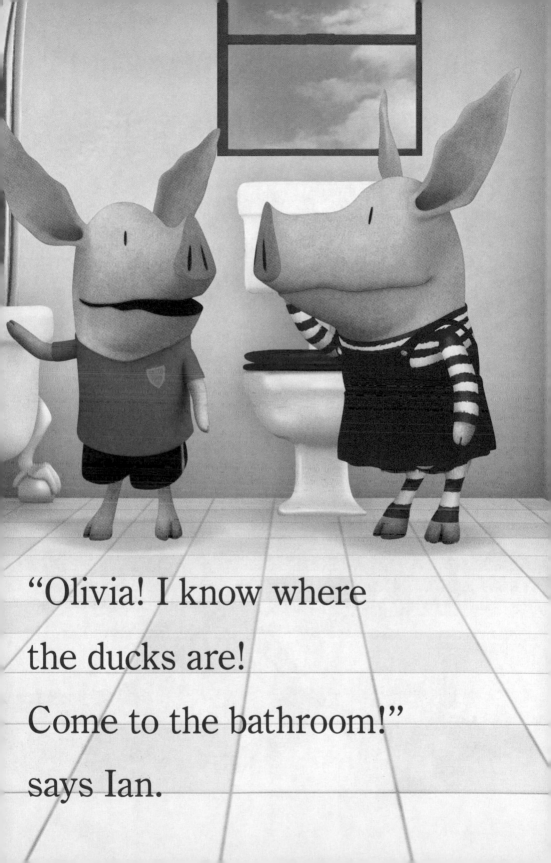

"Olivia! I know where
the ducks are!
Come to the bathroom!"
says Ian.

The ducks are in the bathtub!
"Just because I hate baths
does not mean ducks
hate them too," says Ian.

After their swim,
it is time for bed.
"Would you like me
to read you a book?"
Olivia asks the ducks.

But the ducks are asleep.

"Good night, ducks," says Olivia

Soon Olivia will be asleep too.

OLIVIA™
Takes a Trip

adapted by Ellie O'Ryan
based on the screenplay "OLIVIA Takes a Road Trip"
written by Eric Shaw
illustrated by Jared Osterhold

Ready-to-Read

Simon Spotlight
New York   London   Toronto   Sydney

Olivia and her family
are taking a trip.
Olivia is excited to fly
on a plane!

Olivia packs her trunk.
She packs clothes and
her favorite toy.

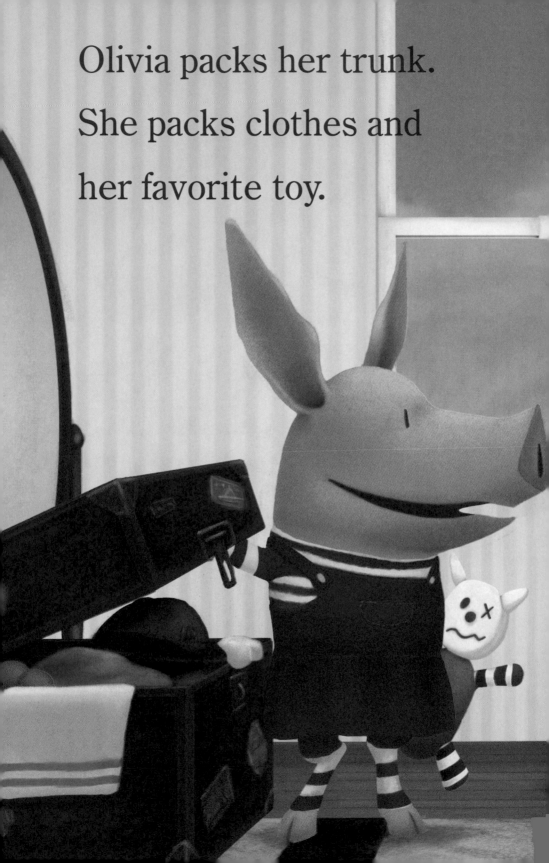

Ian packs a small
lunch box.
"This is my suitcase!"
Ian says.

Dad has some bad news.

A big storm is coming.

The plane cannot fly
in the storm.

They will drive the car
to Grandma's house
instead.

Olivia is sad.

She wanted to fly
on a plane!

Julian comes over
to say good-bye.

He has a present for Olivia.

It is a walkie-talkie!

Olivia and her family
get in the car.

"Are we there yet?" Ian asks.

The walkie-talkie is loud.
It wakes up William!
William starts to cry.

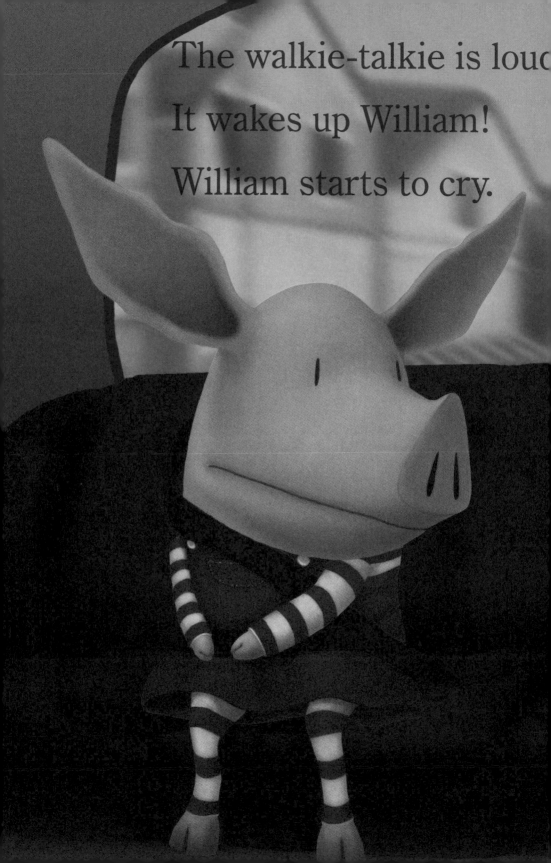

Olivia wishes she were

on a plane.

The car ride is boring.

At the gas station Olivia helps Dad wash the windshield.

Dad's brush has soap on it.

Olivia's brush is muddy.

Dad has to wash the
windshield again!

Mom buys an ice pop for
Olivia and Ian to share.
Olivia wants the red part.
Ian wants the red part too!

The ice pop lands on the car.
Dad has to wash the
windshield again.
"We will never get
to Grandma's house!"
Olivia says.

Olivia has an idea.
She will imagine that
she is on a plane!

"Welcome to Air Olivia!"
Captain Olivia says.

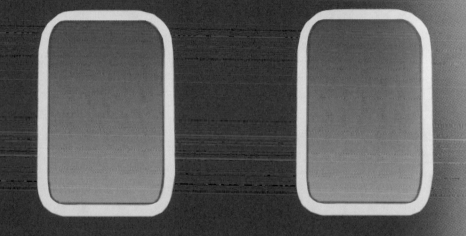

Olivia's plane has a movie
for Dad to watch.
And popcorn for Dad to eat.
There is a yummy dinner
for Mom.

And a red rose for Mom, too.
"This is the best plane ever!"
Mom says.

Captain Olivia tells her family to put on their seat belts.

Captain Olivia sees dark clouds out the window.

"Uh-oh!" says Olivia. "Dark clouds mean a storm is coming."

"We will fly around the storm," Captain Olivia says. The plane loops around a rainbow.

It flies past the storm!

"We are at Grandma's house!" Olivia shouts. She gives Grandma a big hug.

OLIVIA™
Goes Camping

adapted by Alex Harvey
based on the screenplay written by Patrick Resnick
illustrated by Jared Osterhold

Ready-to-Read

Simon Spotlight

New York   London   Toronto   Sydney

Olivia and her family
are going camping.

Olivia's best friend,
Francine, is going too.

Francine does not think
she likes camping.
"I will get dirty and wet,"
she says.

"Camping is fun," Olivia
tells her.
"There are five things you
must do on a great
camping trip."

"Number one: watch my dad try to put up the tent."

"He will forget to put in all the poles.

And the tent will fall
down!"

"Dad always needs my help," Olivia says.

Olivia tells Francine to use
the hammer to bang the
tent stake into the ground.

"Now, the number two thing is to climb a mountain."

"But my foot hurts," Francine says.

"Do you want to lie down?"
Olivia asks.
"I will get dirty if I lie
down," says Francine.
Olivia says that getting
dirty is part of camping.

It is number three on her list.

"But I don't want to get dirty," Francine says.

Francine brought her blanket, pillow, and cot. Olivia brought her sleeping bag.

Number four on Olivia's list: find a really cool bug.

"Ow! I got bitten by a mosquito," Francine says.

"That doesn't count," says Olivia.

"But it itches," Francine says.

"Mud is great for bug bites," Olivia says.

"Eww! I am dirty and wet
and covered with mud!"
Francine cries.
"I need a shower!"

Olivia ties a bag of water
to a tree branch.
Then she pokes holes
in the bag.

Water spills out ...
like a shower!

"Cool!" says Francine.

Olivia tells Francine that number five on the list is to find a perfect stick to roast marshmallows.

"One end of the stick
must be sharp," says Olivia.
"But not too sharp!"

"This stick has too many branches.

This one is too long . . .

and this one is too short."

"How about this one?"

Francine asks.

"Perfect!" says Olivia.
"You are a great camper,
Francine."